wrk
6/22

D1414229

THE TEAM

TAKING
A STAND

Written by Alan Durant
Illustrated by Will Huck

Thanks to Inclusive Minds (the CIC supporting and
championing inclusion and diversity in children's
books) for introducing us to Kay and Gabriella
through their network of Inclusion Ambassadors.

Special thanks also to Harrison, Parker and Reegan.

Badger
L E A R N I N G

Titles in the Making the Team Series:

The Challenge

The Battle

Up and Running

Paying the Penalty

Taking a Stand

The Final

Badger Publishing Limited
Oldmedow Road,
Hardwick Industrial Estate,
King's Lynn PE30 4JJ

Telephone: **01553 816 082**
www.badgerlearning.co.uk

2 4 6 8 10 9 7 5 3

Taking a Stand
ISBN 978-1-78837-659-4

Commissioning Editor: Sarah Rudd
Editor: Claire Morgan
Designer: Bigtop Design
Cover: alphaspirit.it/Shutterstock

TAKING A STAND

Contents

Characters

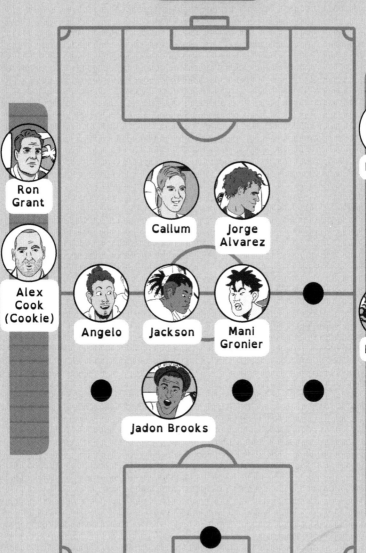

Ron Grant

Alex Cook (Cookie)

Callum

Jorge Alvarez

Angelo

Jackson

Mani Gronier

Jadon Brooks

Bradley

Marissa

Vocabulary

holding midfielder: a player that stays close to the team's defence, instead of attacking

kneaded: to squeeze with the hands

press conference: an interview given to lots of journalists at the same time

pro contract: an agreement to play for a football club in exchange for money

spectator: a person that watches an event

tricky: a player with a lot of different skills

winger: team member that plays in the wide areas of the pitch, that both attacks and defends

But he didn't look fine.

Before lunch, Ron Grant called the three young players to his office. Jackson wondered if this was the moment he was going to announce that he was giving them all pro contracts. But it was about something else. The club had set up a press conference that afternoon and they were going to invite some fans along too.

"Everyone wants to meet you, lads," Grant said.

"Us?" said Angelo. He sounded worried.

"Don't worry," said Grant, "Cookie will be there too to keep an eye on things."

"Sounds great," said Jackson.

Jackson preferred playing football to talking about it, but it was only a few questions, wasn't it?

It couldn't do any harm...

CHAPTER THREE

The conference was in the club's media room. There was a long table draped with a blue cloth and four chairs. Jackson sat on one side of Cookie with Angelo and Callum on the other.

Behind them was a backdrop with the name of the club sponsors and the club badge, which featured a bird. The bird was a kite, which gave the club its nickname, The Kites.

In front of the table, rows of chairs had been put out. All were taken. The room clicked with cameras.

The first question went to the coach:

"So, Alex, you must be very proud of these three young players. Could you tell us what's so special about them?"

"Yes, very," replied Cookie. "They work hard and now we're seeing the rewards. Stanford has an excellent academy, and I expect even more talented players to break through into the First Team soon. Our manager is a big supporter of giving youth a chance."

Jackson recalled that Ron Grant had said the same thing the day he'd called him and four other young players to his office and challenged them to impress him.

Jackson, Callum and Angelo had made it through but the other two hadn't.

Jackson wondered where they were now. How were they coping with having their dreams shattered, after all those years at the club?

If that had happened to Jackson, he didn't know what he would have done.

The next question was for Jackson. It was from a reporter from the national newspaper that Mrs Earls had been reading that morning.

The reporter asked, "Can you tell us, Jackson, how it felt to score the winning penalty?"

Jackson smiled. That was easy enough to answer.

"It was amazing," he said. He paused. "And I owed it to the team after my mistakes in the first half."

Jackson had scored an own goal and given away a penalty in the first half against Milan.

"So, you felt like you needed to make up for the own goal?" the reporter prompted.

"Yeah." Jackson nodded. "I was brought up to believe that if you do something wrong, you should put it right."

"What about when something is done wrong to you?" the same reporter asked. "Racism, for instance. Have you experienced much of that?"

Jackson hesitated. These weren't the kind of questions that he had expected. Cookie sensed his unease and answered for him.

"We have a clear policy on racism at this club," he said. "We don't tolerate it. There's no place for it in our game."

Cookie moved the questions back to lighter subjects:

How did the young players feel about their new stardom?

What was it like to play alongside legends like Jorge Alvarez?

Who were their football idols?

What were their ambitions?

How did their families feel about their success?

The players began to relax. They enjoyed talking about their football careers, the club and the team.

Angelo talked a bit about his Italian heritage. His mum was English but his dad was Italian. He and his family were actually Roma fans, and a group of his Italian relatives were coming over for the final.

"So, who will your family be supporting?" a reporter asked.

Angelo smiled. "Roma, of course. But they'll be happy if I have a good game."

Jackson felt a pang of envy. Angelo's family were coming all the way from Italy to watch him play. Jackson knew that his dad wouldn't come to the final even though he only lived ten minutes away.

If Jackson's dad wasn't working, he'd be playing chess with his friends. He had probably only seen Jackson play a couple of times at most.

Jackson knew it was worse for Callum though. His dad had never watched him play.

Cookie asked for some questions from the fans.

Callum's best friend, who used a wheelchair, put up his hand. Jackson thought his name was Bradley. His speech was a little unclear and Jackson couldn't make out all the words. Callum could, though.

He repeated Bradley's question. "How does it feel to play for the best football team on the planet?" He frowned as if he were thinking hard. "Hmmm, well, it's even better than beating you at FIFA."

There were some laughs from the crowd, and Bradley grinned.

"Well, ladies and gentlemen, we have an important match to prepare for," Cookie said, smiling. "So I think we'll wrap it up there. Thanks for coming and for your questions."

The conference had gone well, but something was bothering Jackson. It was the question that the reporter had asked him about racism. Well, he had experienced it, and very recently.

In the final practice match before the tournament, Jackson's play had annoyed Mani Gronier. The Frenchman had fouled him, but, worse, Jackson was sure he'd racially abused him.

Jackson had learned some French from his early childhood in the Congo, and his parents were fluent. He knew enough to understand some of the things Gronier had said to him — and that they were racist.

Jackson hadn't said anything about it to Gronier or anyone else. He didn't want to cause drama. But maybe he should have?

His dad always said, "You have to speak out about wrongs, especially if you have some power, because then you give a voice to people who don't."

Jackson wasn't sure what to do. He'd stood up to Blake when the gang leader had tried to get information about the players from him. But this was different. He hated Blake.

Mani Gronier was his teammate.

CHAPTER FOUR

Jackson's sister, Marissa, was in the women's squad for a match that evening against Chelsea, the best team in the league. Jackson thought that watching the match would be a good distraction.

Callum and Angelo said they'd join him, and Callum invited his friend Bradley too. He said that Bradley was upset and needed cheering up.

"What's up?" Jackson asked.

Callum took out his phone. He brought up a social media post with a video attached.

"Look at this," he said in disgust.

Jackson watched. It was a video of Bradley at the conference.

The video had been edited so it looked as if Bradley was thrashing in his wheelchair, throwing his head and arms around. In the background was the question he'd asked, but it had been changed so that the words were all jumpy.

"How does it f-f-f-feel?"

At the end of the short video a caption came up on the screen. It read:

How does it feel to be mental?

"That's terrible, bro," Jackson said, shocked. "Who would do a thing like that?"

Callum sighed. "You know how it is with social media. People think they can say anything and get away with it." He frowned angrily. "It's disgusting."

Jackson told Bradley he was sorry about the video when they all met up for the women's match.

"I'm used to it," Bradley said. "People call me all sorts of names. I don't like it, but they're idiots. You can't let them beat you."

"Yeah, agreed," Jackson nodded. "But they shouldn't be allowed to get away with it. Abusing you because you're in a wheelchair or..." he paused, "...because of the colour of your skin."

Jackson told the others what Gronier had said to him in French.

"That's horrible!" gasped Angelo.

"Totally," Callum agreed. "It makes taking the knee a joke, doesn't it, when there's a racist in our own team?"

Bradley was so angry that he clasped the arms of his wheelchair to steady himself. "Someone needs to call him out."

Jackson heard Bradley loud and clear. It was time to take a stand.

CHAPTER FIVE

The Stanford women's team put up a good fight, but Chelsea were too strong. The final score was 4–1.

Marissa came on for the last half hour and did well. She was the youngest player in the squad and Jackson was really proud of her.

Jackson loved watching his sister play. It took his mind off his own issues for a while, but also, it was just nice being a fan again. Cheering on a team and really wanting them to win. Reacting to the highs and lows of a game, not as a player, but as a spectator.

Callum and Angelo said they enjoyed being fans too. Though it wasn't quite the same for them as they didn't have a sister on the team.

"Now you know what it's like for me, watching you guys every game," Bradley said. "So, please, make sure you win tomorrow against Roma..."

"Win against Roma?" Angelo repeated, "We'll do our best."

"And when I score the winning goal," Callum added with a serious look, "I'll come over to you and celebrate and make those social media trolls feel stupid and jealous."

"Yeah," said Jackson, slapping hands with Callum. "And we'll join you."

When Bradley's ride home arrived, Callum and Angelo set off to go back to Mrs Earl's house.

Jackson went into the players' lounge to wait for Marissa.

He stood up and clapped when Marissa appeared.

"Good work, sis," he said.

Marissa rolled her eyes. "Er, we lost, Jackson."

"Yeah, I know," he replied. "But you played well."

Marissa pulled a face. "We need to do better if people are going to take us seriously." Then she smiled. "But what about tomorrow? Playing Roma in the final, that's amazing."

Jackson nodded.

"I just saw Mani Gronier coming out of Ron Grant's office," Marissa said. "He looked furious."

Jackson heart jumped. "You saw Gronier?"

"Yes," Marissa replied. "I think he was heading for the car park."

Jackson took a deep breath. "I need to have a word with him," he said.

He gave his sister a hug and said, "See you tomorrow, sis!"

"Good luck, bro!" she called as he walked to the door.

Gronier was opening the door to his Range Rover when Jackson caught up with him.

Marissa was right. He did look furious.

Gronier turned and glared at Jackson.

"So, you snitched to the boss," he spat. "Now I'm out of the final."

Jackson was baffled. "What?" he blurted.

"You complained to the boss that I said something racist to you," Gronier hissed, "and now he's banned me from playing in the final. I am suspended while he thinks about my future at the club."

Jackson raised his palms in protest. "I haven't said anything to Grant!" He paused and took a breath. "But I should have. What you said to me that day was not okay. It's never okay."

Gronier blew out his cheeks dismissively.

"Bah, it was nothing. I was angry, c'est tout," he said.

Jackson shook his head. "No. It's not nothing. You were being racist. You abused me because I'm black. And if you can't see how wrong that is, then you deserve to lose your place at the club."

Gronier slammed his car door shut, so that there was no barrier between the two players. He took a step forwards, then seemed to change his mind, and stepped back.

"You cannot say anything these days," he muttered.

He opened his car door again and got in.

"So, now, you had better win tomorrow. Good luck, *mon ami*." He gave Jackson a cold stare, adding, "Without me, I think you will need it."

Jackson watched the silver Range Rover — with its flashy MAN1 number plate — drive out of the car park.

He wondered who had told Ron Grant about the racial abuse. But it didn't really matter.

He suddenly felt so much lighter, like when the physio had given him the back massage earlier. But the lightness was inside him.

Jackson felt grown up — not an academy kid anymore, but a professional, a man. He felt powerful, just like his dad had said.

Maybe standing up for himself could help other young black people to do the same. To remind them that racism would never win.

Now he was ready for the biggest challenge of his whole life. Win or lose in the final against Roma, at the end he would stand with his head held high.

Only, he didn't intend to lose...

Further activities

1 Stanford makes newspaper headlines after their match with Milan, with one headline saying, *KO Kids!* Write a newspaper article that describes the match.

2 Callum, Jackson, and Angelo attend a news conference where they take questions from reporters. What questions would you ask the players and what do you think their answers would be?

Further information

French words:

- **c'est tout** = that's all
- **mon ami** = my friend

Enjoyed this book?

Follow the Making the Team journey across all six brilliant stories!